For Jason, my forever friend
~CF

For Anna, with all my love
~BC

LONDON BOROUGH OF WANDSWORTH	
9030 00002 9340 6	
Askews & Holts	13-Dec-2012
JF	£8.50
	WWX0010196/0021

Text Copyright © 2007 by Claire Freedman
Illustration Copyright © 2007 by Ben Cort
Published by arrangement with Simon & Schuster UK Ltd
1st Floor, 222 Gray's Inn Road, London, WC1X 8HB
A CBS Company

Dual language text copyright © 2011 Mantra Lingua
Audio copyright © 2011 Mantra Lingua
This edition 2011 All rights reserved
A CIP record for this book is available from the British Library
Mantra Lingua, Global House, 303 Ballards Lane, London, N12 8NP

www.mantralingua.com

Hear each page of this talking book narrated in many languages
with TalkingPEN! Then record your own versions.

Touch the arrow below with the TalkingPEN to start

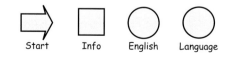

Start Info English Language

Les extra-terrestres adorent les slips
Aliens Love Underpants

Claire Freedman & Ben Cort

French translation by Annie Arnold

Mantra Lingua

Les extra-terrestres adorent les slips,
De toutes tailles et formes.
Mais dans l'espace pas de slips !
Alors voici une surprise énorme...

Aliens love underpants,
Of every shape and size.
But there are no underpants in space,
So here's a big surprise...

Quand les extra-terrestres descendent sur Terre,
Pour VOUS rencontrer ils ne viennent pas...
Ils veulent simplement vos slips,
Je suis sûr que vous ne le saviez pas !

When aliens fly down to Earth, they don't come to meet YOU...
They simply want your underpants - I'll bet you never knew!

Le radar de leur navette spatiale bip
Et clignote à l'instant
Où il voit sur une corde à linge
Des slips dans les airs battants.

Their spaceship's radar bleeps and blinks the moment that it sees
A washing line of underpants all flapping in the breeze.

Ils atterrissent dans votre jardin,
Bien qu'ils n'aient pas été invités.
"Ooooh, DES SLIPS !" ils chantent,
Et dansent en rond, enchantés.

They land in your back garden, though they haven't been invited.
"Oooooh, UNDERPANTS!" they chant, and dance around, delighted.

Ils les aiment rouges, ils les aiment verts ou oranges
Comme des oranges amères.
Mais surtout ils adorent la vue des culottes
Bouffantes de Grand-mère.

They like them red, they like them green, or orange like satsumas.
But best of all they love the sight of Granny's spotted bloomers.

Les culottes roses à dentelle de Maman
Sont un endroit parfait pour se cacher.
Et les caleçons en laine de Grand-père
Font un toboggan super prisé.

Mum's pink frilly knickers are a perfect place to hide
And Grandpa's woolly longjohns make a super-whizzy slide.

In daring competitions, held up by just one peg,
They count how many aliens can squeeze inside each leg.

Dans les compétitions audacieuses,
par une seule épingle tenue,
Combien d'extra-terrestres,
dans chaque jambe sont pendus ?

Ils portent les slips sur leurs pieds et têtes et autres endroits bêtes.
Ils font flotter les slips de leurs soucoupes volantes
Et têtes à l'envers ils tiennent
Des compétitions époustouflantes !

They wear pants on their feet and heads and other silly places.
They fly pants from their spaceships and hold Upside-Down-Pant Races!

Alors qu'ils se balancent dans les airs,
C'est vraiment slip-tastique.
Quel plaisir ont les extra-terrestres
Avec les slips élastiques !

As they go zinging through the air,
it really is pants-tastic.
What fun the aliens can have
with pingy pants elastic!

Ce n'est pas le vilain chien du voisin,
ou les drôles de jeux d'à côté.
Quand les slips disparaissent,
les EXTRA-TERRESTRES sont à blâmer !

It's not your neighbour's naughty dog, or next-door's funny game.
When underpants go missing, the ALIENS are to blame!

But quick! Mum's coming out to fetch the washing in at last.
Wheee! Off the aliens all zoom, they're used to leaving fast...

Mais vite ! Maman vient
enfin chercher la lessive.
Zoum ! Les extra-terrestres s'esquivent,
Ils ont l'habitude d'une sortie vive...

Aussi quand vous mettez vos slips,
Tout fraichement lavés,
N'oubliez pas de vérifier, au cas où
Un extra-terrestre dedans serait resté !

So when you put your pants on, freshly washed and nice and clean,
Just check in case an alien still lurks inside, unseen!